# Ironstone Valley

KU-440-403

**Theresa Tomlinson**

Illustrated by Janek Matysiak

A & C Black · London

# FLASHBACKS

First paperback edition 1999

First published 1998 in hardback by
A & C Black (Publishers) Ltd
35 Bedford Row, London WC1R 4JH

Text copyright © 1998 Theresa Tomlinson
Illustrations copyright © 1998 Janek Matysiak
Cover illustration copyright © 1998 Tom Croft

ISBN 0-7136-4730-2

The right of Theresa Tomlinson and Janek Matysiak to be identified respectively as author and illustrator of this work has been asserted by them in accordance with the Copyright, Designs and Patents Act 1988.

A CIP catalogue record of this book is available from the British Library.

Photoset in 13/19 Linotron Palatino.

Printed in Great Britain by St Edmundsbury Press Ltd,
Bury St Edmunds, Suffolk

# Contents

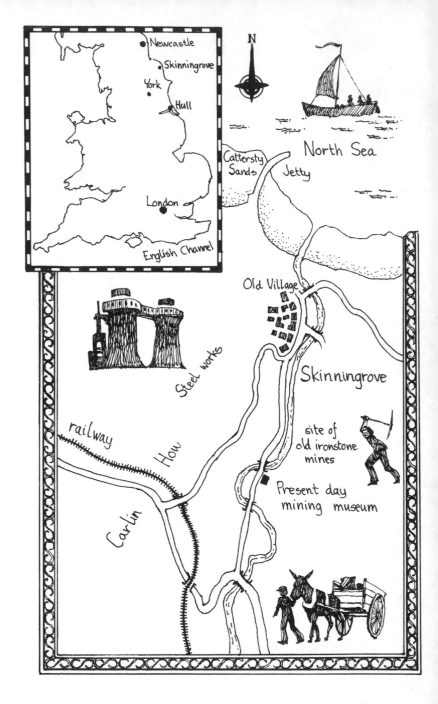

North Sea

Newcastle
Skinningrove
York
Hull
London
English Channel

N

Cattersty Sands
Jetty

Old Village

Steel works

Skinningrove

railway

How

Carlin

site of
old ironstone
mines

Present day
mining museum

# · 1 ·

# Hidden in the Hills

**1865**

Ned Nicholson walked further along the beach, snatching up sticks and throwing them into the basket he was carrying on his back. His shoulders ached as the load grew heavier. He turned and started back towards his mother.

'Mam, haven't we got enough firewood yet?'

Mrs Nicholson bent down to pull a twisted lump of driftwood from a tangle of seaweed. She pushed it into the large basket on her own back, groaning as she straightened up.

'Aye lad, that'll do,' she agreed. 'I can't carry any more. Besides, the tide is coming in, the men will be back soon. Can you manage this big one.'

'Course I can.'

Mam took up the bucket of shellfish and the bag of sea-coal they'd been gathering. Ned grabbed hold of the thin branches poking up from one end of a heavy log that was half-buried in the sand. He tugged and heaved at the driftwood until he

was almost out of breath. At last, it came free. He dragged it over the beach and up the narrow track towards the cluster of cottages that were hidden away in the steep-sided valley of Skinningrove.

As they walked home they could hear in the distance the steady thump of hammers and picks.

'It'll not be long now,' said Mam. 'Not long before they get the railway finished. I daresay we'll be flooded out with all the extra workers they're bringing in to open up new tunnels.'

'Aye,' said Ned. 'Josh Wetherall says he's going to work in the mines.'

Mam shook her head. 'His father won't have that. We're fishing folk, not ironstone miners.'

'Isaac and Tom say the same,' Ned whispered.

'I'd keep quiet about it if I were you.' Mam spoke sharply.

As they passed by where the beck ran into the sea, Mam stopped to rest her load for a moment. 'It was just here,' she said, 'that I met young Mr Maynard and Mr Okey, all those years ago.'

'How long ago?' Ned asked. He'd heard this story many times, but he never tired of it. His mother had been there on the great day that changed everything.

'Eighteen years since,' his mother told him. 'I know it was eighteen years ago, for Mary Ann was a little baby strapped to my back.'

'The day they found the ironstone?'

Mam nodded. 'They were shouting and yelling, two young men with their arms full of rock, splashing across the beck, soaking their good clothes.'

'Did they tell you?' Ned asked. 'Did they tell you what they'd found?'

'Oh, aye. They were that excited they couldn't keep quiet about it. Young Mr Maynard even kissed me, and he stuck a great lump of rock in front of my nose. 'Bless you, Mrs Nicholson,' he said. 'This is ironstone that we've found in the cliffs. It's going to make our fortune!'

Ned giggled. 'And what did you say?'

Mam shook her head. 'I said nowt. I couldn't believe those lumps of muck could make anyone's fortune, least of all ours. They opened up a tunnel, but they never managed to make much money. I still doubt it will make our fortune, even though they *are* bringing the railway right round here.'

# · 2 ·

# Folk Need Fish

Mary Ann and Hannah were sitting outside the thatched cottage that was their home, cleaning Dad's fishing lines. Young Robbie was playing marbles at their feet.

'Have you done?' Mam asked.

Mary Ann pulled a face and stretched as she answered, 'Nearly.'

'That's good,' said Mam putting down the bucket. 'Here's mussels and limpets that we've picked. You can start baiting up the lines as soon as we've had our tea.'

Mam went inside and got the fire going under the little stone-built oven. Then she set a fine-smelling fish stew cooking on the hot bakestone.

'Neddy, lad,' she called. 'Run down and keep a lookout for us!'

Ned didn't need telling twice. He ran down to the sea and stood there skimming pebbles. The wind was blowing straight off the sea, making his hair stream back from his face.

It wasn't long before he saw some dots in the distance. The dots soon turned into four brown triangular shapes – the sails of fishing boats.

Ned ran back to the cottages.

'They're coming. They're coming,' he shouted.

'Good lad. Tell Mrs Wetherall will you?'

'I heard you, honey!' Mrs Wetherall from next door came out, pulling a shawl around her shoulders.

Out from the tiny cluster of cottages came a small gang of women and girls, all hitching up their skirts and tucking them into their waistbands as they headed for the sea. Young lads raced ahead of them, stamping on to the gritty shingle beach.

The boat nearest the shore was *The Bluebell*. Ned splashed eagerly into the water, waving his arms until his father flung the rope to him.

'Got it,' Ned yelled, and fell full length into the water. Bubbles rose all round him as he quickly righted himself.

'Eh, dear our Neddy,' his dad laughed.

Ned struggled out of the water, dripping wet.

'Still got it,' he cried, waving the rope.

'You're a good lad,' his mother told him, trying not to laugh.

She took hold of the rope and began pulling her husband's boat in to shore. Nat Nicholson and Ned's older brothers, Tom and Isaac, jumped out into the water in their long leather sea boots, and set about hauling the sturdy fishing boat out of the water and up on to the beach.

All the neighbours joined in, some wading into the sea, others grabbing the rope. Soon, with a great deal of heaving and groaning, *The Bluebell* was dragged up beyond the high-tide mark.

Later that evening, when they'd finished their tea and Dad had lit up his pipe, Tom and Isaac began talking, as they did every night now, about the new mine owners and the coming railway.

'Josh Wetherall says the Pease family are willing to take on local men,' said Isaac. 'He says he's off to see the new manager on Saturday.'

Nat Nicholson listened quietly, puffing away at his pipe and shaking his head as they spoke.

'Could there be better money to be earned?' Tom wondered.

'I doubt it very much,' Dad growled. 'Local men! What do local men know of mining? Fishing is our business. Fishing is what we know! Folk need fish and we must get it for them.'

# · 3 ·

# Bloater

They were up with the sun next morning. Mam made them all a drink of tea before Dad and the boys went off in the boat. Ned loved walking down to the sea to see them off, but Mary Ann grumbled all the way. Dad laughed and kissed her, trying to cheer her up.

'Come on, honey,' he teased. '*You* are our special girl.'

Mary Ann sighed. Only girls who were called Mary Ann were allowed to help push out the boats each morning. Any other woman might bring bad luck and foul weather. And as for a pig! If a fisherman on his way to sea saw a pig loose – he might as well turn round and go back to bed.

When they returned to the cottage, Hannah was setting off to the donkey field, a strong rope halter in her hands.

'Is it us today?' Ned asked.

Hannah nodded and pulled a face. 'Will you come and help me?' she begged.

'No fear!' said Mary Ann.

'I'll come,' said Ned. He followed her up to the field at the bottom of the steep grassy hillside they called Carlin How. Bloater the donkey lived there and was shared by the small fishing community. Each family took turns at harnessing him to the wooden cart and leading him up the cart track to sell fresh fish in Loftus market. Bloater was their prize possession, but he was bad-tempered. First, he had to be caught!

Hannah pulled a handful of carrot shavings from her apron pocket.

'You hold them out to him,' she told Ned. 'I'll be ready with the halter!'

They climbed the wooden fence, Ned waving bits of carrot. Bloater was quickly tempted but, with a sharp twitch of his head, he snatched the carrot peelings and galloped off, kicking up his heels at the sight of the halter.

'Stupid moke!' Hannah shouted. Bloater, munching noisily, watched them from a distance. 'Has he got it all?'

Ned nodded.

Hannah sighed. There was nothing for it but to chase the beast around the field. It wasn't long before they were both exhausted, and Bloater hee-hawed wildly.

Hannah was close to tears.

'Give it to me!' said Ned, holding out his hand for the rope halter.

'Go on then, Clever Dick!' Hannah said as she handed him the halter.

Ned crept towards Bloater, clicking his tongue the way Mam did when she was angry. The tough little donkey rolled his eyes and moved away – but not very far. He seemed puzzled by the strange sounds. Ned tried again making noises a bit like the swish and lap of the sea on a calm day.

Hannah held her breath.

'Swish, swish,' went Ned.

Bloater looked at him still puzzled, but interested. This time he didn't rush off as Ned moved closer. Slowly, and carefully, he slipped the halter over Bloater's head and nose.

'Swish, swish,' Ned whispered right in Bloater's ear, then led the donkey meekly out of the field.

'I don't know why Bloater seems to like our Ned,' Hannah told her mother resentfully, when they got back to the cottage.

Mam smiled. 'Some folk have a useful way with beasts. Let's hope our Ned is one of them. It's grand to see the cart all fixed and ready.'

'Well,' said Hannah, laughing, 'with a name like Neddy, he should be good with donkeys.'

Autumn turned to winter and all through the hardest months, work continued on the railway. Life in the tiny hamlet struggled on.

Mrs Wetherall started coming round to the Nicholson's cottage whenever it was her turn to take the donkey cart.

'Can I borrow your Ned?' she'd say. 'There's nobody can catch that stubborn beast like he can.'

One blustery spring morning, Mr Pease drove his pony and trap down into the valley, followed by two other pony carts.

'Mam!' cried Ned. 'Come and see the gentlemen!'

Mrs Nicholson left her washing and came to look.

Mrs Wetherall brought her knitting outside and stood watching as her needles clicked away. 'Now what?' she murmured.

The men walked up and down the valley bottom. Some of them wore suits, some were in good working clothes. They examined the rock face, cutting small samples with their chisels.

Mr Pease paused and touched his hat politely to the fisherwomen. 'The railway is almost finished ladies. We're going to open up a tunnel in the valley side.'

They all blushed, bobbing curtseys.

'There's miners coming up from Cornwall to start the work, ladies. They'll be needing lodgings and food. There'll be plenty of money to be made.' Mr Pease touched his hat again and walked back to the carts. Mam and Mrs Wetherall stared after him.

'How can we give lodgings?' said Mam. 'We hardly have room for ourselves.'

Mrs Wetherall shook her head. 'I don't know what my Daniel will have to say about it.'

# · 4 ·

# *The Little Melody*

None of the fishermen liked the idea of sharing their homes with strangers. But Mr Pease didn't let that put him off. The carts came back piled high with wood and thin sheets of iron. The workmen set about building shacks close to the beck.

Ned watched it all with interest, and so did his mother.

One day, a cart full of miners arrived. Their jackets and breeches were worn almost thread-bare and the way they spoke sounded strange. They climbed out of the carts all stiff-legged and tired. The soles of their heavy boots had iron studs that sparked and scraped as they clambered over the rocks.

With them, came another cart piled high with picks and shovels. Behind that came another, driven by Kitty Kildale who sold hot pies in Loftus market. Everyone knew Kitty. She was a big strong woman who shouted all the time.

Kitty's pies were infamous all over Cleveland. There were plenty of jokes made about her name.

Mam would wink and say, 'She should be called Kitty Kill'em, I say!'

Ned watched as Kitty unloaded stacks of wooden bowls and spoons. She made herself a little camp and soon had a huge pot, bubbling away above a fire.

'They're queuing up for bread and stew,' Mary Ann told her mother. 'They're paying money for it!'

'Here, Neddy lad,' said Mam. 'Go and see how much they're paying, but don't let them know what you're up to.'

Ned ambled over to the men and returned shortly with the news that they were paying a penny for a bowl of stew and a hunk of bread.

'The bread looks hard,' he told her. 'And the stew is like watery porridge.'

Mam wrinkled her nose and looked at the girls. 'We could do better than that!' she said. 'We could brew up a lovely tasty fish stew with onions and potatoes, and still charge the same.

'Aye, we could,' said Mary Ann. 'And Mrs Wetherall's oatcakes are the best for miles.'

But when they suggested it to Dad that night,

he shook his head stubbornly, and said, 'It's fishing for us.'

So, Mam watched impatiently as more men arrived, and Kitty Kildale raked in the pennies. The miners set to work opening up deep tunnels in the hard cliff of the valley. All day long, the clunk of metal on rock could be heard.

## 1867

It was the day of the storm that changed everything. Skinningrove fishermen always had a hard time with high spring tides, but it was years since there had been a storm like the one that came soon after Easter.

The fishermen set off early one morning with the sea as smooth as silk, but by noon the sky had turned dark and the sea choppy.

'I don't like it,' Mam said. 'I'm going down to watch for them!'

Mam was not the only one who was bothered. As the wind grew, all the wives and children came pouring out of the cottages. They found it hard-going for the fierce wind nearly blew them over. With the lashing rain stinging their faces, they struggled down to the beach and stood there worried sick about their men.

'There,' cried Ned. His sharp eyes had spied the boats. 'They're coming.'

'Thank God,' Mrs Wetherall whispered.

'Oh no!' Mam shouted. 'They're too far over. They're heading for the rocks.'

The women and children shouted and waved, trying to give warning, but the roaring of the sea drowned out their cries. For a moment they all fell dreadfully quiet. They watched helplessly as the Wetherall's boat, *The Little Melody*, was dashed hard against the rocks.

Poor Nelly Wetherall gave a terrible wail, then the watching women and children went stumbling into the wild sea. It was bitterly cold and strong currents caught at the women's soaked petticoats. They struggled on towards the boats, desperate to give help.

'Hush, Nelly,' cried Mam. 'I can see them. They're hauling your Daniel aboard *The Bluebell*.'

'Yes,' yelled Ned. 'Father has got hold of Mr Wetherall. He's safe now.'

'But what about our Josh, can you see *him*?' Nelly cried.

Ned could not answer her, for the small boats had vanished behind the torrent of fierce waves and beating rain.

'Have they got our Josh? Have they got my lad?' Nelly begged, but nobody could give her an answer.

A cheer went up as *The Bluebell* came back into sight and began to lurch shoreward. It bobbed wildly up and down, dragging the smashed hull of *The Little Melody* behind it. The women waded into the deep water towards their men. Then, suddenly and wonderfully, extra help came.

A great gang of men were splashing into the sea beside them. The Cornish miners had thrown down their picks and shovels and rushed to their aid. And now there were many willing hands to haul *The Bluebell* ashore.

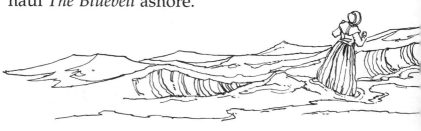

'Where's our Josh?' shrieked Nelly Wetherall as she grabbed hold of her husband's freezing oilskins.

Daniel Wetherall turned his face away in sorrow. He could hardly speak. 'I'm sorry, mother,' he whispered. 'We've lost our lad.'

Mam grabbed hold of Nelly and pulled her back. She hugged her tight. 'Let your Daniel be, honey.' She spoke gently but firmly.

Mam made Nelly come out of the sea. They stood a long time in the howling wind, wanting, praying that the sea would give back the Wetherall's beloved son. But there was no sign of him. Eventually, Mam dragged Nelly back to the cottages. Mr Wetherall followed them slowly, head down, leaving the others to finish hauling the boats up on to the beach where they would be well out of reach of the raging sea.

# · 5 ·

# After the Storm

All that afternoon while the storm raged, Mam and Mary Ann quietly set up lines inside the cottage to dry the miner's clothes along with their own. Though he was full of sorrow and anger about Josh drowning, Mr Nicholson invited Tinner Samson and Cop Trevorrow to sit by the fire and take a sup of ale with him.

'We are most thankful for your help,' he told them.

'We're sorry for your loss,' Tinner Samson said.

'Don't blame yourself,' Cop Trevorrow tried to soothe Mr Nicholson. 'You couldn't have done more. That was the grandest bit of seamanship I've seen since my father's days.'

Once they'd got used to the strange way the Cornishmen spoke, they found they had plenty to talk about. Cop Trevorrow came from a Cornish fishing family and he knew all about the risks of riding the spring tides.

'What made you take to mining?' Dad asked.

Cop looked sad. 'My father was drowned, and my older brother with him. Our boat was smashed beyond repair.'

Mr Nicholson nodded, understanding only too well.

'So, I took myself off to the copper mines,' Cop told them. 'But now those mines are closing and every man in our company has lost his job.'

'Ah,' said father. 'So, now you come as far as Skinningrove, looking for work.'

That night when Cop and Tinner got up to go, Mr Nicholson cleared his throat and suggested that, as the storm still raged, they might care to stay the night.

Mam was surprised. 'You're most welcome,' she added. 'Though I don't know where you are going to sleep.'

'The lasses can sleep on the floor in our room,' said Mr Nicholson firmly, 'the lads, up in the loft.'

Mary Ann and Hannah smiled. They did not object.

The visitors feasted on fish stew and dumplings for their supper. Next morning they came downstairs to a bowl of Mam's steaming hot porridge. They ate heartily and by the time they'd finished, their bowls were scraped clean.

'Never tasted porridge like it,' Tinner Samson told Mam.

She laughed and blushed.

And that was how Tinner Samson and Cop Trevorrow came to lodge with the Nicholson family. They stayed the night and never went back to their shacks.

The cottage was cramped but Mam set up a wickerwork screen to divide the bedroom. Dad made a wooden cupboard bed for Ned, so that he could sleep nice and warm by the kitchen fire.

Three days later Josh's body was washed up at Staithes. Not long after the funeral, Nelly and Dan Wetherall bravely invited two of the Cornishmen to lodge with them.

Other villagers offered their homes as lodgings, and soon, instead of having to drag the fish cart up to Loftus, the women used the catch to feed the miners. Kitty Kildale was furious. She packed up her bowls and pans and left the valley.

Mr Nicholson took Dan Wetherall out fishing with him in *The Bluebell* until Dan could decide what to do about the poor smashed up *Little Melody*.

One evening soon after the storm, Tom and Isaac went next door to speak to Mr Wetherall. An hour later, the three of them came back to the Nicholson's cottage, all looking solemn.

'What's up?' Dad asked.

'*The Little Melody*,' said Dan, 'she'll never mend. Now, I know you aren't going to like it, Nat Nicholson, but I think you should listen well to what these lads have to say.'

'Well?' said Dad. 'Get on with it!'

Isaac took a deep breath. 'Cop says the manager is wanting young fellows for the mines. We want to go.'

Nat Nicholson frowned and waved his pipe at his eldest son. 'What do you know of mining?'

'Doesn't matter,' said Tom. 'Cop and Tinner will teach us. They just need strong men, willing to learn.'

'And who's going to sail with me?' Father folded his arms. 'I can't handle *The Bluebell* alone!'

'I will,' said Dan. 'If you'll let me. We'll break up *The Little Melody* and use her to repair *The Bluebell*.

Mr Nicholson thought for a moment, then he sighed and nodded sadly. 'Aye,' he agreed. 'There's sense in what you say, but we'll not be a fishing family any more.'

# · 6 ·

# Donkeyboy

Dad and Mr Wetherall still went off fishing in *The Bluebell*, but the Nicholson family did become more of a mining family. What Mr Pease had told Mam proved to be true. There was money to be made, but for the miners the money was small and the work very hard. Mam and the girls washed and cooked and scrubbed to look after the miners, and still they had the fishing lines to clean and fix. By the afternoon, they were exhausted and they hardly had time to sip a cup of tea before Mam would be shouting, 'They'll be back soon! Build up the fire!'

The miners all came home with boots and trousers soaked with dank muddy water. Whenever it was fine Mam would set up bowls of warm water in the yard for them to wash in. Sometimes, the men were so weary after their work that they needed help peeling off their trousers and pulling off their boots. Mam would see to Tom and Isaac, while the girls were glad to roll up their sleeves and help the Cornishmen.

'Heave ho!' shouted Mary Ann, as she pulled off Cop Trevorrow's boots.

Hannah always went to help Tinner Samson.

The sour-smelling work gear was set to steam by the fireside. If they were lucky, their things would be just about dry before they started the next shift. Dad liked to sit by the fire in the evenings, talking with the Cornishmen while Mam and the girls worked away at their knitting.

'Stories!' Ned begged. 'Tell us stories!'

When his father told his tales, Ned would drift off to sleep in his cosy cupboard bed, dreaming of storms, shipwrecks and mermen; but when it was the Cornishmen's turn, he dreamed of rock falls deep in the ground, or mine pixies that lived in deep dark tunnels and tapped and screeched and played wicked tricks.

Time passed – the railway was finished and working, and more miners came to Skinningrove. They came from Wales and Lincolnshire, from Norfolk, Sussex and Essex. They came with their wives and children from any place where men were hard up and short of work. Pease & Partners began to build neat rows of cottages along the valley sides. More and more tunnels were opened and tubs full of ore were sent to Middlesbrough. It seemed the ironstone seam stretched for miles around.

Tinner and Cop were made pit deputies. It was their job to keep the tunnels shored up with timber to make them safe for the work. They earned a steady wage that way, and Cop married Mary Ann. Hannah planned to marry Tinner, but her father said she was too young and must wait until she was eighteen. Mary Ann didn't move far away, for her father and Cop built on another two rooms at the side of the cottage. Mary Ann and Mam could each sit on their own doorstep and chat in the evenings.

When Ned was ten he told his mother, 'They're all earning money. I'm going to earn some too.'

'What!' said Mam. 'You're not going in that mine!'

'No,' Ned agreed. 'Not yet! I'm going to make old Bloater work with me.'

Mam nodded her head. 'Now then, just you take care!'

So, Ned earned pennies by leading Bloater and the donkey cart up and down the valley, carrying waste shale to the tip, snout ends of timber, picks and shovels, or anything else the miners needed shifting. He soon earned himself the name of Donkeyboy.

On fine Sundays, Bloater had to share his field with the twelve magnificent shire horses that hauled the heavy tubs of ironstone through the dark tunnels and out of the mine. The horses worked hard all week but on Sundays they were set free. Ned would creep into the stables and fill his pockets with oats, then he'd sit perched up on the fence, watching with shining eyes as the great beasts snorted and galloped about the field. He loved to hear the thunder of their hooves.

# · 7 ·

# The Trappy Lad

**1867**

One spring afternoon when Ned was just turned eleven, he was loading snout ends of wood into the donkey cart close to the gaping entrance to the tunnel they called the North Drift. He stopped for a moment and watched as the shift finished and weary miners came staggering out into the bright afternoon sunlight.

'Donkeyboy! Over here, lad,' Cop Trevorrow called, coming towards him waving a scrap of smudged paper above his head.

Ned left Bloater and ran to him. He snatched the paper from Cop's hand.

'This it, then?'

'Sure it is,' said Cop. 'Overman Easton says you can start Monday, at six!'

'Hooray!' yelled Ned.

Cop shook his head. 'I hope you know what you're doing.'

'Course I do! Anyone can be a trappy lad! All

you've got to do is open doors!'

'There's a bit more to it than that, lad.'

But Ned wouldn't listen. He ran back to Bloater, waving the paper under the donkey's nose. 'I'm a trappy lad now,' he bellowed into Bloater's twitching ear. 'Robbie will have to see to you now, old fellow.'

Once Bloater was back in his field, Ned ran home to show the paper to his mother. Mrs Nicholson had just swept the kitchen floor and was sprinkling clean sand over the stamped-down earth so that all would be clean and nice for Sunday. She stopped when Ned came running in, and her eyes went all watery as she realised what the paper meant.

'What's wrong?' said Ned. 'I'll be working like a man. I'll be bringing home a proper wage, not just the odd penny.'

Mam sniffed and tried to look pleased. 'Aye,' she said. 'I shall have to make you a fine big jam sandwich to take with you, won't I?'

Ned rushed off to find Robbie. Saddened to think of Ned in the mine, Mam watched him go, then finished sprinkling sand over the floor.

Ned could not sleep on Sunday night. He was excited, but now that the time was coming close he was scared too. Although he had passed those holes in the cliff face many times, he had never once been inside the mine. He'd seen his brothers walk up there in the mornings, and watched as they strode in and were swallowed up by the darkness.

Ned knew well enough that the mine brought danger as well as hard work. Tinner and Isaac had once carried Tom home after a runaway tub had crushed his leg. Ned remembered Tom's blood-soaked breeches and the awful groaning that went on all through the night. Mam had staunched the blood, cleaned the wound and nursed Tom back to health. He still walked with a limp, but Tom thought himself luckier than some. The men had once struggled to get Frank Metcalfe out when he'd been caught by falling stone and timbers, but by the time they reached daylight, he was dead. Ned remembered the slow tread of the miners as they carried poor Frank up to his mother's cottage on the bankside. He thought of the sadness that was always there in the old lady's face.

# · 8 ·

# Into the North Drift

When Ned's mother came down to build up the fire in the morning, she found Ned still awake.

'That may be just as well,' she said. 'You can be dressed and ready before the men come down. Now then, I've got some things for you.'

Mam pulled an oilskin bundle from the bottom of the cupboard. Ned smiled with pride as she brought out a clean pair of heavy working boots with steel nails and plates hammered into the soles. 'They'll be a bit big,' she told him. 'But they've not had much wear. I got them from Mrs Metcalfe. Her Frank can't use them now and she was glad of the pennies I paid her for them. See what else!' She held up a fine pair of thick knitted stockings. 'I've been rushing to get them done in time. I unravelled our Robbie's old jumper.'

Ned didn't much like the idea of wearing a dead miner's boots, but he took them and the stockings. 'Thank you, Mam.'

'Matches,' said Mam. She carefully counted

out twelve, and put them into a box for him. 'Don't you waste them.'

When the men came down, they put on their stiff, dry work clothes and drank a mug of tea that Mam had ready for them and ate a bowl of porridge. Then Mam gave them each a small wicker basket that contained two good hunks of bread sandwiched together with sweet bilberry jam, and a corked stone bottle of tea. The men were working in tunnels that stretched far into the hillside, which meant they couldn't come back for their midday dinner. But, they loved Mam's bilberry jam and they called their food parcels their bait.

Ned took up his basket and followed the men to the North Drift.

When they got there, the men filed quietly through a wooden hut, each picking up a midge. The midge was a small metal box with a handle on top and an open front. A stubby candle was fixed inside, stuck down with clay.

'Take up that midge!' Cop told him. 'But don't light it yet.'

Ned did as he was told.

'Right,' said Overman Easton. 'New trappy lad, isn't it? Name?'

'Ned Nicholson, Sir.'

'Nickname?' the overman asked.

Ned wasn't ready for that, even though he knew the miners all had nicknames. Tom was Hopalong or Hoppy, and Isaac was Stewpot, for the miners had never forgotten Mam's fish stew.

'He's Donkeyboy,' said Cop.

'Of course he is,' the overman laughed. 'I hope he isn't stubborn as a mule. Take him to Top Door, District Five.'

'Walk behind me,' said Cop.

At that moment, Ned would have given anything to be back leading the donkey cart round the village. But then he remembered the money he'd be getting at the end of the week and pushed those thoughts away. He followed close behind Cop and the darkness closed in all around them.

# · 9 ·

# District Five

They trudged on down the tunnel, and Ned looked back at the fast-shrinking half-circle of daylight behind him. When he turned around again, the tunnel seemed darker than ever. Ned slowed up. He couldn't see where he was putting his feet, though Cop marched on as fast as ever. At last, they came to a wooden door that neatly fitted into the arched shape of the tunnel. Cop pulled it open.

'Is this my door?' asked Ned.

'Nay lad, we're nowhere near yet.' Cop sounded amused.

Once through the door they took a sharp right turn.

'Along here,' said Cop. 'We call this the inbye tunnel, for it takes us in. You shall have to come out a different way.'

'Outbye?' asked Ned.

'That's right. A tunnel that takes you out.'

Ned had often heard the men talking of inbye and outbye. 'How do I find outbye?' Ned asked.

It seemed to him that, since they'd turned the corner, they were walking in the pitch dark.

Cop's voice sounded strange and echoey. 'Don't fret. I shall come and fetch you out. We don't expect you to find your own way. Not first day, anyway. Come on, we'll light up now.'

Ned was very glad when Cop struck a match and lit both their midges. The light they gave was small but at least he now had some idea of the tunnel walls and where he was putting his feet. Slowly, he became aware of a faint crack of light ahead of them, and muffled sounds of voices. Cop reached the place and pulled aside a thick sacking curtain, letting shimmering candlelight spill out into the tunnel.

'Cabin,' Cop told him. 'Have a look.'

Ned stared open-mouthed into a small room cut out of the rock. It was crammed with men, most of whom he knew well.

'Now then,' said Cop. 'Here's our Donkeyboy!'

'Hey up, Ned!'

Isaac and Tom were there, sipping tea from their bottles while it was still warm.

'Shall I be near my brothers?' Ned asked, comforted a little at the thought.

'Aye, we'll not be far away,' Tom told him.

Isaac ruffled his hair. 'Best get to your door,' he told him. 'We'll be at work soon and sending the tubs through. What if there's no lad to open the door for them?'

Ned was sorry to turn away from the rough friendliness of the cabin, though he felt better knowing that it was there. Cop set off fast down another tunnel, then round a sharp left turn, then a right. They passed two more trappy doors. At one, Biff Barker who Ned knew well was swigging his tea.

'You starting on the doors?' he asked.

'Yes,' Ned told him, hoping he sounded braver than he felt.

'Best of luck,' Biff muttered as they passed through his door.

The mine was criss-crossed with straight tunnels and Ned was dizzy with trying to remember how many turns he'd taken. At last, Cop slowed down. Ahead of them in the gloom Ned could see another wooden trappy door.

'Top Door, District Five,' said Cop.

'Is this it?' asked Ned.

'That's right. You know what to do?'

Ned put down his midge and tugged at the door. It came open quite easily. 'Like this?' he asked, holding it open.

'That's grand. Now close it, and keep it closed till a tub comes. It keeps the good air in place.'

'How will I know when a tub's coming?'

Cop laughed. 'You'll know, laddie. Now, I must be off. Sit down there and make yourself comfortable. You've a long wait. I'll come for you when the shift is done.'

'All right,' said Ned shakily.

Cop went on through the door. 'Blow out your candle,' he called back.

'What?' Ned called after him in panic.

'Blow out your candle!' Cop repeated, his voice growing faint. 'It won't last the whole shift.'

# · 10 ·

# Pixie

Cop was gone and Ned was alone. The thought of blowing out the candle was terrible. It was the only scrap of comfort he had. He wasn't going to blow it out yet.

Ned looked about him in the shadowy glow of his candle and found a small hollow hewn out of the stone where he could crouch. He put down his basket, then sat and waited.

Longing to hear a friendly sound he thought he heard the distant sound of hooves. He jumped up and went to the door but all was quiet again.

Ned sat down and waited for what seemed an endless time. Nothing happened, though he did hear muffled sounds of blasting and a few creaks and shuffles. Time went by and he got very cold and hungry. He remembered that he'd got his *bait*. Surely it must be dinner time by now. He unwrapped his sandwich and took a bite. Mam's bread and bilberry jam tasted heavenly. Somehow the taste of it gave him courage. He could see that his candle was shrinking fast, so he took a match in one hand, ready to strike when needed, and held his sandwich in the other. Then he gritted his teeth and blew out the candle.

Ned had never known such black-velvet darkness. He couldn't see anything. He could not even see his sandwich. He couldn't see his hand in front of his face.

He sighed. So this was it. This was what he must get used to. It almost felt as if he were floating in a sea of pitch. Only the cold damp rock beneath his backside told him that he was still safely on firm ground. It was a very lonely kind of darkness.

As he sat there clutching his bread for fear of losing it, he thought he heard scuffling and a small squeaking. Ned's heart began to beat very fast. He thought something brushed past his feet. He froze.

Yes! He felt it again.

Suddenly, there was a tug at the bottom of his breeches.

Ned held his breath. Cop's stories flooded into his mind. Pixies that knocked and screeched and played tricks. Wicked pixies that led poor miners into danger. He could not bear it. Ned leaned back and felt for the hard ironstone rock behind him. Though his hand shook, he managed to strike one of his precious matches against it.

In the flare he saw two bright eyes looking up at him. His heart missed a beat, then all at once he understood.

It was a rat, up on its back legs, its nose twitching and snuffling.

Just a rat! Feeling foolish Ned lit his midge candle. He was used to rats. His mother often called him in to chase them out of the house. He sat there staring down at it and the rat again reached up and tugged at his bootlaces.

'What's up?' he whispered, feeling silly. Though he'd spent hours talking to Bloater, only a fool would talk to a rat.

The rat squeaked and tweaked his breeches. Ned stuck his finger into his sandwich and brought out a smear of bilberry jam. He held it out to the rat. It nibbled like mad, loving the stuff, then it squeaked and tugged at his sleeve wanting more.

Ned laughed. This place was so strange and lonely that even a rat seemed a better friend than none at all.

He blew out his candle. This time the warm furry
body brushing against his ankle brought comfort.
He broke off a tiny piece of sandwich and smiled
as tiny sharp teeth tickled his hand.

'I'll give you a nickname too,' he whispered.
'I'll call you Pixie.'

# · 11 ·

# **Duchess**

Ned fed scraps of his sandwich to the eager Pixie, but, suddenly, the creature pricked up its ears and scuttled away into the darkness of the tunnel. Ned was puzzled for a moment, wondering what had scared it, but then he heard the distant clopping of hooves. Was this a tub coming at last?

The sounds grew louder. Yes. A horse and tub were definitely coming down the tunnel towards Top Door, District Five. Ned leapt up, dropping the remains of his sandwich, his hands shaking. He scrambled over to the door and yanked it open. He could hear the 'Yar! Yar!' of the driver lad and the squeak and clank of the tub's wheels. Ned peered through the door and saw the dark mass of the horse approaching with the shaky light and shadows of the driver's midge as he walked behind.

Ned pulled the door back as far as he could, panicking at the thought of the horse's great bulk being too big to get through it. But, suddenly and wonderfully, the great Clydesdale mare was there, ducking her head so that her powerful shoulders fitted through the opening perfectly.

'Duchess!' Ned yelled.

Duchess snorted a friendly greeting and blew a gush of warm horsey breath into Ned's face.

'Gerron!' the driver yelled.

It was Stoney Bates who was a few years older than Ned. He was called Stoney for the accuracy of his aim with a catapult. More than once, Ned had felt the sting of Stoney's shot on his behind.

'Close it quick or I'll sprag yer!' Stoney yelled at him, pointing with his short iron bar. 'Yar! Gerron Duchess!'

By the time Ned had the door securely closed again, they were fast vanishing into the darkness.

'Woa!' Stoney yelled. And Ned heard a loud clack as Stoney threw his iron sprag into the tub wheels to slow Duchess down. They'd be gone in a moment.

'Hey, Stoney!' Ned shouted. 'Is the shift nearly finished?'

Stoney's laughter echoed back to him. 'Nearly finished? We've only just got going,' he said.

Ned curled up by his door again, dismayed.

He picked up the gritty half sandwich that was left and tried to clean it. He'd better save it for later if Stoney had told him the truth, but you could never be sure with Stoney. Ned felt as though he'd been down there for a full day already. He carefully wrapped what was left of his sandwich in the cloth and put it back into his basket, then uncorked his bottle and took a swig of tea. It was still slightly warm. Stoney had been telling the truth.

Ned settled down to wait again. This time when he blew out his candle he was ready for the thick darkness. Time certainly seemed to move very slowly in this featureless underground world.

Three more tubs came quite close together. Ned was kept busy. It felt better having something to do and knowing other folk were nearby. Then there was another very long wait. He grew so hungry that he could not hold back from eating the rest of his sandwich. He shared scraps of it with Pixie. Each time he blew out his candle and settled in the quiet darkness, he did not have to wait long before the urgent tug at his bootlaces came.

'Hello, fellow,' he whispered, putting his hand

down to touch the sleek, warm body.

Though it was cold, Ned grew sleepy in the long waits between tubs and he was nodding off when at last, Cop came back for him.

'Hey there, trappy lad!' shouted Cop laughing. 'Shift is over! Time to go home.'

'Thank goodness,' whispered Ned.

Cop led him through an outbye tunnel, back to the entrance to the North Drift, and out into the sharp afternoon sunshine. Ned could not stop blinking and rubbing his eyes. His back and shoulders felt very stiff.

When he stumbled into his own yard, the other men were already there washing themselves and he caught the strong smell of soap coming from the kitchen. Of course, it was Monday. Mam would be busy with her washing, just when he was so hungry he was ready to drop.

Ned crept past the men into the kitchen and slumped down on a stool by the fire. He wasn't going to bother getting washed. Not yet, anyway. He sat there surrounded by damp, dripping shirts, too stiff and cold even to speak. Mam took one look at his pale smudged cheeks and went to the pot she'd been boiling whites in. She fished about with a wooden spoon and brought out a small oilcloth parcel fastened tightly with string.

Ned's eyes opened wide with hope

'Now then, what have I got in here?' Mam teased.

She untied the parcel and tipped the contents out into a bowl. It was a hot suet pudding that had been boiling away with the washing all day. Mam spooned bilberry jam over the steaming delicacy, before handing it to Ned.

'Now then, that'll set you up!'

'Oh, Mam,' said Ned. 'I do love you!'

# · 12 ·

# Digger Welford

Ned struggled through the first week of work. He was mightily relieved when Sunday came and he got his day of rest. The following months were hard, but Ned learned fast. He grew used to the long, lonely waits in the dark with only a rat for company, and looked forward to the moments of excitement when the horse tubs came. Ned soon knew each horse by name and most of them snorted a friendly greeting as they passed through the trappy door. All except Hector, who was muzzled because he was a biter.

After a few mistakes, Ned learned by heart the pattern of dark passages that led him to and from District Five. On one occasion when he wandered in the wrong direction, he found a wonderful, whitewashed, horsey smelling place with stalls full of clean moss litter and brown peat bedding.

Digger Welford looked up from the barrel of chopped hay and oats he was mixing. 'Where did you spring from, lad?' he asked.

'I was looking for outbye,' Ned told him.

Digger laughed. 'Well, what you've found are the underground stables!'

At the sound of clopping hooves Digger left the barrel and unfastened a chain that had been slung across the entrance to one of the stalls.

Stoney came round the corner leading Duchess, free of her tubs at the end of the shift.

'Hold on a minute!' said Digger, 'and I'll fill her trough.'

Stoney had a job holding on, for Duchess had got the scent of the fresh choppy mix of hay and oats and wanted her dinner there and then.

Ned reached up to stroke her nose. 'Cush! Cush!' he soothed, just as though the huge mare was Bloater. Digger shovelled hay and oats into her feeding trough while Ned and Stoney tried to calm her.

'Thanks,' said Digger, slipping out of the way. 'Good thing you were here, lad. I could do with a helper like you. Ready now!'

Stoney let go of the bridle and Duchess headed for her dinner. She didn't need leading towards that.

Ned followed Stoney through the outbye

horse tunnel, till the bright, glowing eye of daylight could be seen ahead.

'Could I be a driver lad?' he asked.

'Nay,' Stoney told him. 'You've got to be twelve, at least, and you've to be good with a sprag.'

'Show me!' Ned demanded. 'Show me how to sling a sprag!'

Stoney shook his head. 'Clear off, trappy lad! Don't you think I've got enough to do?'

But Ned was not going to be put off so easily. 'I'm going to be a horse driver,' he told Isaac and Tom that evening as they all sat round the kitchen table in clean shirts, tucking into stew and dumplings.

Tom pulled a face and shook his head. 'Slinging them sprags is the devil's own work,' he said. 'How many drivers have still got all their fingers?'

'Stoney Bates has,' said Ned. 'Anyway, is losing a finger worse than crushed legs?'

Isaac grinned. 'He's got you there, Tom,' he said.

Ned had to be patient and carry on working as a

trappy lad. A year passed and by the time spring came again, Ned had become used to the hard life. Through the winter he went to work in the dark, sat all day in the dark of the tunnel and went home in the dark, too. Digger Welford did not seem to mind if he wandered into the stables at the end of his shift. Even though he was cold, hungry and stiff, he found the energy to sit polishing the brass and black leather bits and bridles while Digger told stories of the cleverness or wickedness of the various horses he kept.

'Oh, yes,' said Digger. 'These horses know exactly what they are doing. Old Hector, there, goes and fits himself between the tub shafts. He doesn't need telling! But he'll have an oatcake out of your pocket like lightning as soon as his muzzle is off!'

Sundays brought a blessed relief. Ned, all washed, brushed and in his best clothes, would follow his family up to the little chapel on Carlin How bankside. He dozed through the preaching but loved the singing. Sometimes, he bellowed out the hymns so loudly that Mam gave him a little dig in the ribs. After the service they returned home for the wonderful feast of Sunday dinner. Even if they'd lived on fish tails all week, there would be a good roast joint of meat on Sunday. Then, while Mam and Dad dozed by the fire, Ned and his brothers walked out on to the heather-topped hills that surrounded the valley.

It was the best time of the week. Ned's stomach was full for once and, even when the weather was cold, at least he could breathe sparkling clean air.

Isaac and Tom would have liked to take *The Bluebell* and go out fishing, but father wouldn't hear of it – not on a Sunday. Instead, they went up on to the hills to set snares for rabbits. Ned learned to sling a net to catch fat pheasants and partridges, to tickle trout and to avoid the Duke of Zetland's gamekeeper. The brothers helped themselves to game, mushrooms, nuts, berries or poached fish. They never returned home without something tasty for Mam's pot.

# · 13 ·

# A Broken Prop

One Saturday afternoon in late summer, Cop came tramping down the tunnel to District Five. His deputy's lantern swung about, making wild shadows jump on the walls.

'Shift finished?' Ned asked

'Aye,' Cop answered wearily.

'I'll come with you then,' said Ned, snatching up his basket.

'Nay,' Cop told him. 'They're complaining of a broken prop in District Six. I'm waiting for Taff Lewis and the new deputy so that we can check it before we go home. You go ahead, I shouldn't be long.'

Ned didn't argue. He knew that checking props was important. He strolled home, delighting in the warmth of the sun on his back.

Mary Ann was standing by her back door with her baby, Jack, in her arms.

'Sunday tomorrow!' yelled Ned, tickling the baby under his plump chin.

'Get your hands off!' Mary Ann lifted the baby high above her head, making him gasp and dribble. 'I've got him all clean and you're filthy.'

Ned peeled off his damp muddy clothes and washed himself out in the yard. He rubbed himself dry and went inside to put on a clean shirt before sitting down with his brothers to eat boiled crabmeat and oatcakes. It was only when Isaac and Tom were lighting up their pipes and talking about going down to the sea to look for Dad, that Ned went back out into the yard.

Mary Ann was still sitting there on her doorstep. She looked worn out and little Jack was fretting as she rocked him to and fro.

'Cop not back?' Ned asked.

Mary Ann shook her head. 'No, he's not! The bairn won't settle and Cop's tea is spoiled.'

As Ned sat there in the sun, rolling clay marbles beside the step, he began to worry about Cop. He started to feel rather sick and wished he hadn't eaten so much crab. He didn't want to frighten Mary Ann, but his own worry was slowly growing. Dealing with broken props could be dangerous, but he knew Cop wouldn't be alone. The deputies always worked in threes.

At last, Ned dropped his marbles and got up. 'I'll go to the North Drift and look for him,' he said.

He strolled out of the yard but, once outside, he ran to the mine. He pelted towards the lamp cabin, reaching it just as Overman Easton was coming out. He was looking worried, too.

'Now then, Donkeyboy?' he said.

'Have you seen Cop Trevorrow?' Ned gasped out.

'Aye, I have seen him and I'm getting a bit bothered about him. He was impatient to get home and wouldn't wait for Taff and the new fellow. He went looking for broken props in District Six.'

'By himself?' Ned was shocked.

The overman nodded. 'I told him not to.' He turned back to the lamp cabin and ran his finger along the row of metal tallies that told him who was in the mine and who had come out and gone home. 'There's Digger still in there, and Stoney. I'm surprised at that, he's usually first out on a Saturday night.'

Ned could not stay patient. 'There's something wrong!' he shouted. 'I'm sure there's something wrong, Mr Easton.'

'Aye.' The overman lit a lantern and snatched it up. 'Come on, lad, we'll find out fast as we can!'

They marched into the tunnel, then started to jog, stumbling and tripping where the ground was rough. Just as they reached the turning for District Six, the overman slowed down. Ned was going so fast he crashed into him.

'Hey up!' Mr Easton chuckled, pointing ahead. 'Here he is!'

The distant light of a lantern swung about as a figure moved fast towards them.

'Thank goodness,' said Ned with relief.

They stopped and waited by the turning as the light came closer. Ned had a moment of doubt. He knew Cop's bobbing walk very well and it wasn't him.

'That's not Cop,' he said. 'That's Digger.'

'Aye. So it is.'

They could see from Digger's face that he was worried too.

'Hector's not back,' he told them. 'His driver's smashed his ankle, and Duchess has got foot rot, so I had to send Stoney out with Hector, even though they don't get on. I've waited since the end of the shift, but there's no sign of them.'

'Where were they working?' Overman Easton asked.

'District Six,' said Digger.

# · 14 ·

# Hector

Without another word, all three took the sharp right turning away from the main tunnel and started running towards District Six. Before they turned the last corner they could hear the muffled neighing and snorting of a horse in distress.

Stoney was shouting frantically. 'Gerrup, Hector! For God's sake, gerrup!'

As they turned the corner, Overman Easton grabbed Ned by the arm and slowed him down, 'Steady now, lad,' he said. 'We don't go charging in, whatever has happened.'

Ned's heart was pounding and his hands were shaking, but he did as he was told. He could see the sense in it.

The overman went ahead carefully, holding his lantern high. What they saw filled Ned with fear. A broken prop had fallen across Hector's back and the terrified horse was down on his knees. Stoney was trapped behind, trying to lift it, frantically urging the horse to get up.

'Quiet!' Overman Easton told him sternly. 'Quiet, lad. We'll do our best to get us all out.'

It was Cop who bothered Ned most. The Cornishman had wedged himself in at the side. He was supporting a cracking timber prop with his back. Ironstone crumbled and slipped down between the roof timbers, threatening to fill the tunnel. Cop did not attempt to speak but they could hear his harsh breathing.

'You keep back, lad,' said the overman to Ned. He set down his light and slipped in beside Cop.

Digger went to help lift the broken timber from Hector's back. 'Come on now, old fellow,' he coaxed gently. 'Come on now, get up! There's room. You can do it.'

Hector whinnied and champed his great teeth, but he would not move. The enormous bulk of his body shuddered.

'Come on, Hector! Get moving!' Digger's voice turned sharp with urgency. He had to jump aside as a lump of ironstone slipped out from behind the broken timbers. It clipped the side of the tub and grazed Hector's back leg as it fell to the ground. The horse snorted and neighed wildly, shaking his head and rolling his eyes.

Ned could no longer stand back. He reached over Hector's damp neck to loosen the bridle, then slipped off the restricting muzzle, trying not to think about the strong yellow teeth.

'Just pretend it's Bloater,' he told himself.

He stroked the massive head. It was wet with sweat and gritty with crumbling stone and mud.

'Cush! Cush!' he soothed. 'Cush! Cush!'

Hector shook his head again and rolled his eyes, but he did not bite.

Cop still said nothing, but a low groan came from his lips.

'Swish! Swish!' whispered Ned, his mouth close to Hector's ears. He made all the soothing sea sounds that Bloater loved so much.

'You're doing well, lad,' said Digger, his voice low and steady again. 'Now then, come on Hector. Up you get, boy!'

Hector dipped his head and struggled to raise himself. Ned soothed and stroked steadily. He did not even pull away when the great teeth snapped at him.

'Swish! Swish!' he urged.

Suddenly, in one strong movement, Hector was up and the tub was moving. Digger threw the broken prop aside and went to catch Hector's bridle. A tear-stained Stoney followed fast.

'Thank God,' whispered Cop.

'I'm never,' Stoney sobbed, 'never going in with that horse again.'

# · 15 ·

# Get Out!

Digger did not stop. He quickly led Hector and the tub up the tunnel towards safety, with Stoney running close behind.

Ned wanted to run too, but he could not leave Cop.

'Get going!' Cop hissed at him. 'Get going, so we can come after you!'

Only then, did Ned do as he was told and start backing along the tunnel.

'Are you ready, Cop?' Overman Easton whispered. 'Right! NOW!'

Both men ducked down and hurtled full pelt towards Ned.

'Keep going,' Cop shouted.

Ned went fast. He ran for his life.

Sharp cracks like pistol shots told them the timber had broken. A great rumbling sound came next as crumbling ironstone and shale slithered down from above, then deafening thunder as the tunnel roof caved in.

Ned ran on. Cop and Overman Easton were right behind him. Thick dust choked their lungs and filled their eyes but, at last, they reached the main tunnel of the North Drift

A small crowd had gathered as word spread that something seemed to be wrong. Mary Ann came marching into the tunnel with Jack still in her arms.

Isaac followed. 'No,' he shouted. 'It's unlucky for a woman to go into the mine!'

Cop flung his arms around his wife and child. 'Not if she's called Mary Ann,' he shouted, crying and laughing with relief. 'You should know that!'

Mary Ann hugged him tight, for once not caring that she and the baby were covered with grime.

There was a great deal more laughter and many tears. Ned walked over to Digger.

'Is Hector all right?'

'Aye, he is lad. Thanks to you. He needs a good feed and a brush down, but his cuts and bruises will soon mend with a bit of liniment rubbed into them.'

Overman Easton came to speak to them. 'You did right well in there, lad,' he told Ned. 'You've a grand way with horses. I'm thinking that you're wasted on the trappy doors. Would you like to be a driver?'

Ned's face lit up. 'I would,' he said, 'but I'm only just turned twelve, and I'm not much good with a sprag.'

'Don't worry! You will be!'

Ned turned around, surprised. It was Stoney who'd been listening to what was being said. 'I'll show you,' he said. 'I'll teach you to sling a sprag better than anyone else in the mine.'


Stoney kept to his word. Every spare moment he had he spent up by the field with Ned, practising slinging a sprag.

'You have to get to be a dab hand out in the open daylight first,' Stoney told him.

'All right,' Ned agreed.

Stoney turned out to be a strict teacher, determined that Ned was going to get it right. First, they slung sprags at the broken tubs piled up in the yard, then when Ned had become a really good shot, they ran beside the tubs that carried the ironstone to the railway.

'Sprag your tub, Mister?' they'd shout to the

drivers. Then they'd sling the iron bar in between the spokes of the wheels, whether the driver wished it or not.

By Christmas, Ned was a fully-fledged driver, the youngest in the mine. Digger gave him Hector to drive. The great heavy horse was gentle with his new master and was soon free of his muzzle. They became a famous team.

# Epilogue

**1926**

Ned sat on Carlin How bankside, looking down on Skinningrove and the rows of little houses that now filled the valley. Behind him up on the brow of the hill was a big steel works with blast furnaces, sheds and chutes, and wooden slatted cooling towers. More rows of houses clustered around the works.

Ned's hair was now white and thin, and his back was stiff and achey. He was seventy years old. Beside him, sat his seven-year-old grandson, Eddie

'Tell me again, Grandpa,' said Eddie. 'Tell me about Duchess and Hector and the other horses.'

Ned smiled. There was nothing he liked more. Others in the valley had heard his stories so often they were bored with them, but for young Eddie the stories were fresh and new.

'Well...' said Ned. 'When I was sixteen, the bosses made me deputy stableman. I worked in the stables deep inside the mine with Digger Welford, and I learned how to treat the horses when they were sick.'

'Tell me about greasy heel, Grandpa!'

Ned chuckled. 'Oh aye, greasy heel! That's a nasty stinking infection that mine horses get. You have to soak the bad places in strong medicine, then scrub at it with a long-handled brush.'

'Horrible!' Eddie shuddered. 'What else did you do?'

'I clipped their manes and tails and combed and brushed them till their coats shone. I fitted their heavy shoes and trimmed their hooves. Best times of all was Sundays and holidays. We'd take them all out into the bright daylight and set them loose in the field. You never saw anything like it. Huge, heavy beasts that they were, running and jumping like spring lambs.'

'How many did you look after?'

'Well, at one time there were ninety of them – when the steel works got going up here on the hillside. The Pease family bosses built the houses, and the school and the cottage hospital.'

'Ninety horses?' Eddie gasped.

'Aye,' Ned nodded. 'The year I turned thirty, they put me in charge of the whole stableblock. We soon had forty-five horses in the main stables, and forty-five inside the mine. We changed them round so they got a bit of a rest.'

'Was it a good job, being stableman?'

'Oh, yes.' Ned spoke with pride. 'The bosses always said, "If a man's injured you can soon replace him, but you have to pay a lot for the right horse." Sad that, isn't it? In some ways the horses were more valuable than men!'

'I want to be a stable lad!' said Eddie. 'When I leave school.'

Ned shook his head. 'Horses are a lot of hard work lad! Still, all the jobs in the mine are hard work. My brothers slaved away for years, fetching out those tubs of stone. Only Robbie followed my father, so at least we kept one fisherman in the family. I always knew I'd rather be with the horses. Better the stables than being tossed about on the freezing sea; or blasting away in the tunnels, breaking your back with shovelling stone and breathing in all that muck.'

'Why do the miners do it?' Eddie asked.

Ned looked puzzled for a moment, then he smiled as he recalled his father's words.

'Folk need iron,' he said. 'And we must get it for them.'

# Author's Note

Mr Okey, Mr Maynard and the Pease family were all real people. Everyone else in the story is fictional. However, they represent a huge workforce that lived and settled in the area of the Cleveland ironstone seam in the latter part of the nineteenth century.

In writing this story, I have drawn a great deal of information from both *Ironstone Mining in Eston*, a personal account by W E Brighton, and *Cleveland Ironstone Mining* by John S Owen.

I would also like to thank Mr Alan Chilton and the dedicated volunteers at The Tom Leonard Mining Museum, Deepdale, Skinningrove, for their help, advice and encouragement.

# Glossary

**beck**        A stream.

**inbye**       A tunnel leading in towards the workings of the mine.

**outbye**     A tunnel leading out from the workings towards the exit of the ironstone mine.

**overman**    The man in charge of workers in each **shift**. He is also the link person between the miners and the mine manager.

**moke**       Local name for a mule or donkey.

**shift**        A specific period of time worked by a group of workers.

# Further Reading

Now you have read *Ironstone Valley,* you might like to read more about life in the nineteenth century, at a time when the Industrial Revolution was changing every-thing. Here is a selection of the many books available.

**Fiction**

| | |
|---|---|
| Theresa Tomlinson | **The Cellar Lad**, *Red Fox* |
| Walter Unsworth | **The Devil's Mill,** *Victor Gollancz Ltd* |
| Jill Paton Walsh | **The Butty Boy,** *Puffin* **Thomas and the Tinners** *Macdonald Young Books* |
| Catherine Cookson | **The Nipper**, *Macdonald* |
| Leon Garfield | **December Rose**, *Puffin* |

**Non-fiction**

| | |
|---|---|
| John D Clare | **I Was There: Industrial Revolution,** *Bodley Head* |
| Penelope Davies | **Children of the Industrial Revolution, An Eyewitness History Book**, *Wayland* |
| Dorothy Turner | **Victorian Factory Workers, Beginning History** series, *Wayland* |
| Jason Hook | **Stephenson and the Industrial Revolution, Life and Times** series, *Wayland* |